FORBIDDEN DESIRE

SCARLETT FINN

I0743632

Also by Scarlett Finn

NOTHING TO...
NOTHING TO HIDE
NOTHING TO LOSE
NOTHING IN BETWEEN: ONE
NOTHING TO DECLARE
NOTHING TO US
NOTHING IN BETWEEN: TWO
NOTHING TO SAY
NOTHING TO GAIN
NOTHING IN BETWEEN: THREE
NOTHING TO YOU
NOTHING TO THIS PREQUEL: ONE WILD NIGHT
NOTHING TO THIS
NOTHING IN BETWEEN: FOUR
NOTHING TO DO
NOTHING TO FEAR
NOTHING IN BETWEEN: FIVE
NOTHING TO DENY

GO NOVELS
GO WITH IT
GO IT ALONE
GO ALL OUT
GO ALL IN
GO FULL CIRCLE

KINDRED SERIES
RAVEN
SWALLOW
CUCKOO
SWIFT
FALCON
FINCH

EXILE
HIDE & SEEK
KISS CHASE

THE EXPLICIT SERIES
EXPLICIT INSTRUCTION
EXPLICIT DETAIL
EXPLICIT MEMORY

THE FORBIDDEN NOVELS
FORBIDDEN DESIRE
FORBIDDEN WANT
FORBIDDEN WISH
FORBIDDEN NEED
FORBIDDEN BOND

WRECK & RUIN
RUIN ME
RUIN HIM

MISTAKE DUET
MISTAKE ME NOT
SLEIGHT MISTAKE

THE BRANDED SERIES
BRANDED
SCARRED
MARKED

TO DIE FOR...
TO DIE FOR TRUTH
TO DIE FOR HONOR
TO DIE FOR VIRTUE
TO DIE FOR DUTY
TO DIE FOR LOVE

RISQUÉ & HARROW INTERTWINED
TAKE A RISK
FIGHTING FATE
RISK IT ALL
FIGHTING BACK
GAME OF RISK

FORBIDDEN PREQUEL DUET
ALL. ONLY.
ONLY YOURS

LOVE AGAINST THE ODDS STANDALONE COLLECTION
SWEET SEAS
HEIR'S AFFAIR
RESCUED
MAESTRO'S MUSE
GETTING TRICKY
THIRTEEN
REMEMBER WHEN...
RELUCTANT SUSPICION
XY FACTOR

LOST & FOUND
LOST
FOUND

ONE

"MISS… MISS…!"

Even over the music, Sersha McLeod heard him shout the first time. Not responding was a choice. Good sense. A defense mechanism. A woman sitting alone at a bar in such a busy nightclub was a target. Better a target at Stag than prey at home.

"Hey!"

The shouter appeared in front of her, forcing her attention away from her phone. Two of them, actually, dressed in black, a red stag head on each of their collars. So, right, not lubed partiers ready to hit on her, employees. And from their substantial build, she'd say more likely security than bar or maintenance staff.

"Yes, gentlemen?" she asked, taking a shot at a smile. She just wanted to be left alone. Apparently, that was too much to ask. "Is something wrong?"

Bars flanked tables and booths on the upper section of the split-level club. The one to the right of the entrance was her preference, her regular perch. Music blared from the furthest corners. Scores of bodies jumped and danced on the lower level. None escaped the pound of the bass.

"You've been invited upstairs!"

Upstairs? Better than the opposite.

Licking her lips, she did a deliberately bad job of hiding her smile. At least she was polite enough to dip her chin and let her eyes flash up to his in coy flirtation. A rebuff always landed better with a little ego stroking.

"Thank you," she said, skimming her hand across the bar to touch the stem of her glass. "I appreciate the invitation…" The guys were too relaxed to know what would come next. In fact, the one behind took a semi sidestep, anticipating she'd rise from her stool. She wouldn't. "But I decline."

Guy One didn't register. Guy Two did something of a double take before his colleague turned and they made eye contact. A shrug followed a bewildered blink. Was rejection really so unusual? Yes. The owner of this club would be used to getting his way.

Giving them a second to gather themselves, she picked up her martini glass to sip and moisten her throat. So much for Stag being a safe bet. Just what was it about her that drew the interest of these mob men? Was a little peace too much to ask?

"We, uh…" Huh, Guy One had lost his bluster. "You should really come with us. You want to come with us."

"I don't," she said. "An invitation implies choice. I choose to refuse. I don't want to meet your boss. I don't want to talk to him. I don't want anything to do with him."

Maintaining her smile was another tactic. These kinds of guys, the hired muscle, they were used to conflict. Used to hostility. They would deal with defensive or angry using aggression and violence.

No sirree, she did not want any part of that.

Polite, disarming, unthreatening weren't so much their purview. Keeping them confused was her only chance of escape.

"Oh… kay."

Maybe they were new. Or maybe she really was the first to spurn a great McDade monolith. Okay, so she wasn't. An earthquake had gone through the family not long ago when a McDade uncle and cousin were imprisoned. Somehow, the McDade empire emerged stronger and stretched further than it ever had. Even if it was lighter a few men at the top.

The goons once again shared a look. This time when one moved, the other followed and they shuffled off. Good. Peace. It wouldn't last. No was not a word their boss would receive well. Inhaling, she blew out her breath slowly, absorbing the remnants of the social atmosphere. Safety was about to slip from her fingers.

As her shoulders dropped, she finished her drink and tucked her phone into her clutch. She needed to find a cab. Not as she liked to, amid the melee of a hundred other people forced out when the club closed in the early hours. No, alone, probably while some eager wannabe clubbers still lined up behind the red rope outside waiting for their chance to sink into Stag.

Sad that she'd have to say goodbye to such a beautiful place. The ceiling towered over the vast cavern. The other floors took up only a fraction of the footprint of the space. What was up there on the second floor? Was there a third? Hmm, it looked like it. No. Stop, Sersha. She didn't want to know. She could hazard a guess, but that wouldn't win her any friends.

Another thing she wasn't great at.

Stop being so cynical. Bitter, that was how her ex put it. Maybe he was right. Maybe the world jaded her. After seeing so many of the horrific things humans could do to each other, wasn't skepticism inevitable?

What a life.

Slinking off her stool, there wasn't much else to do but leave. Could be a no wouldn't offend a McDade. Perhaps she would be able to come back tomorrow and the slight would slide on by.

Yeah. And pigs may fly over a frozen hell.

If a McDade hadn't extended the invite, she could be okay. Maybe it came from a captain or soldier rather than the don. The Irish families didn't have the same structure as the Italians. Who else would have the authority to invite her upstairs? Stag was the domain of one man. The hub from which he conducted business. Not that she wanted details. No, one mafia family on her ass was enough. If a second got a whiff of her? Forgetaboutit, she'd start a war without victors.

Winding through the tables, the passage to the front entrance contained the coat check and admission booths. The regular Joes paid and got a ticket to run through a machine before even getting as far as the metal detectors.

Beside those was the exit. Also known as the direct entry route for anyone who didn't pay or go through a metal detector. The VIPs. A few feet inside, an enclosed staircase led… somewhere. The second floor. A mystery. Sometimes the curtains were closed over it, other times they tied the drapes back. Either way, two guards always flanked that ingress. No prizes for guessing who lorded over everyone from the elevated vantage point.

Damn her curious nature. Staying out of trouble was supposed to be her goal. Why did she have to be so damn inquisitive? Mysteries existed to be solved. Unknowns supposed to become knowns.

She didn't know what was good for her. No, she did, she just cast that knowledge aside when it came to satisfying herself. Learning felt good. Being in the know was enticing. It aroused her. Yeah, okay, maybe that was a salacious way to put it but—

Someone stepped out of the shadow of the staircase into her path. She had no choice but to stop and hadn't so much as looked up when he moved to let another man descend. A third. A fourth. They kept on coming…

Oh, okay. Glancing left and right as the thugs encircled her, the message was clear. Rejection wasn't an option. Was the asshole upstairs compensating for something, or did he believe a show of strength would loosen the elastic of her panties?

"I'm supposed to go up because he won't go down," she said to none of them in particular and sighed. Dropping her cheek closer to her shoulder, her eyes drifted to the side. "Nothing like a man who starts as he means to go on." She set her sights on the closest guy. "Let me guess, he has something really important to tell me… or something really impressive to show me?" She shielded her mouth with the back of her hand to stage whisper, "Spoiler alert, unsolicited dick pics are never appreciated, online or in-person." The two in front grabbed an arm each as the others moved forward, carrying her in a wave to the stairs, a lot of stairs, and upward. "Use your words, boys."

It didn't matter. They didn't speak. Nothing good waited for her beyond the door above.

TWO

THE DOOR OPENED from inside. Thrust into muted warm lighting, she tossed her hair from her face to take in what she could. Curtain over the corner opposite the door. Vacant desk. The men pushed and prodded her to the center of the round black rug with its red stag head emblazoned in the middle.

"I'm going to guess he's overcompensating," she said.

To the right, dull gold frames held together an arch of windows in the wall. Had they been there a while? Maybe. She didn't know the history of the building and the distressed look was in. Could be nouveau vintage.

The banker's lamp on the huge wooden desk, covered in a scatter of papers, was unlit. Why was it so dark? What did he have against illumination? Light came from hidden recesses in the ceiling. And, most notably, from a stag head crest emblazoned on the wall behind the desk.

A snicker snuck around her lips as she looked back to the chesterfield nestled in the nook created between the stairway and window walls.

"This guy has a mirror over his bed, doesn't he?" she said. No one responded. Most of the soldiers were filtering out down the stairs again. "Is his bed shaped like a stag head too?"

Still nothing.

The curtain in the far corner moved and a guy appeared. More than six feet tall, well-built… Did she know him? No… Her eyes narrowed. The unknown guy looked back the way he'd come. Yep, the big reveal was on her horizon.

Two big, thick thugs stayed by the door to the stairs after it closed. Mr. Unknown held the curtain and stepped out the way as his compadre entered.

Oh, yes. Connel "Ire" McDade. Exactly who she expected.

His short temper got him that nickname. Legend surrounded this guy…

Six four, ripped, stubble on the square jaw. Hair black as the night, short at the sides, longer on top; somehow perfect despite looking only finger-combed… Slacks, jacked—uh, jacket, shirt, top three buttons undone.

And the eyes… stories were told about them too. About how he enticed women and cut men down with that laser-precise gaze. From where she stood, they looked as dark as his hair… but, by all accounts, they were green… Hmm, who would tell her something like that? Maybe it was in one of the zillion police reports she'd read.

"Did I insult you?" he drawled.

Oh, shit, why hadn't someone told her about the voice? How was it so deep? Thick like molasses, yet smooth like the wisp of satin between her thighs. Shit.

Why did she go there? What did her panties have to do with anything?

"You were born on the island," she said, tucking her purse under her arm. "I heard that about you."

"Was I?" he asked, strolling toward his desk.

"Mm hmm," she said. A whisper of an accent still tainted his Americanized tone. "You were raised there for your first five years or something. Your mom's a native... was a native..."

Maybe reminding him of his mother's death wasn't a smart idea.

Sinking into the seat, he relaxed with such easy repose, it was clear fear didn't often visit him. "You didn't answer my question."

"Did you insult me?" she asked. "I don't know. Who were you talking to and what did you say?" He didn't so much as blink. Her head tipped toward the two guys by the door. "Your men are a reflection of you... and your values." If a McDade had any of those. "You probably don't hear it often, but sometimes no really does mean no."

"You meant it?"

"I did," she said, and twisted a shoulder in the guys' direction again. "So if I could be excused..."

Like she was back in school or something. Men made the rules around there... Sometimes it felt like they made them up as they went along. Not that she could judge anyone for acting on impulse.

"You've been in my club every night for a month."

"I didn't know anyone was keeping track." No one in that room anyway. "Have I hit my quota?"

"Why?"

"Why have I been in your club every night for a month?" she asked. His finger rose to his cheekbone, supporting his head with the elbow on the chair arm. The slightest movement of a nod confirmed her question. "Did I win a prize?" Each of the guys at the door and the third still by the curtain got her attention for a few seconds. "Don't you want repeat customers? I don't keep a tab. I pay cash every night."

"Woman like you shouldn't be carrying cash in this neighborhood."

"In any neighborhood," she said in agreement. "I have my reasons."

"Tell me."

Her next exhale was almost a laugh. "You're kidding me, right? What do you care?"

"What do you have to hide?"

"I'm not hiding anything," she said. "But I don't owe you a damn thing." Wow, okay, defensive wasn't a good stance. She eased off the gas. "Look, if you don't want me coming back, I won't come back. This is an easy fix."

And boy had she misinterpreted the invitation upstairs. Now she almost wished sex was his motive. Drawing the attention of the McDades, the suspicious of nefarious motives attention, was dangerous. No one would care who her daddy was before she was butchered and strung up. After, maybe, but what would she care? She'd be dead. Dead was never a good outcome.

"What's your name?"

So cool… The aloof attitude didn't bother her. Except it sort of did. Her lower back prickled in a really weird way. One she didn't like. Her hips wanted to move in response to it, to sort of squirm against the vibration of his brogue in the air as it carried to her. It made her itchy and tense. Keep calm. Chill. Deep breath.

Nausea tumbled low in her belly.

Answering his question could either free or kill her. Fifty-fifty odds weren't the kind to play with in a room like this.

"Do you want me to leave?" she asked.

"I want you to tell me why you visit here every night."

"The music is good," she said. "I enjoy being around people."

As one corner of his mouth twitched, he licked his lips and turned his chair just a fraction to look at the guy by the curtain.

"Lies easy."

"They always do, Ire," Curtain Guy said.

Whoa, boy, Curtain Guy was Irish too. Not Americanized Irish like his boss, his accent was the full deal. How did people go about their business around that accent?

McDade rolled himself in at the desk. "Take her to the basement."

"Wait…" she said when the other three men started toward her. "The basement? I know about the basement…" She held up both hands, but the duo of goons grabbed her anyway. Curtain Guy walked around to nudge her toward the exit from behind. "About the people taken down there who are never seen again…" Fighting the grip on her arms, she tried to dig her heels in and resist Curtain Guy's insistence. "About the things you do to people, the disfigurement… how you torture women for your sexual pleasure…" Dropping her weight, she yanked left to right, determined to get away from her assailants. On the threshold of the stairs, desperation freed the truth. "Vex! I'm here because of Evander Manzani!"

"Hold."

The brogue again. The guy at her back stepped aside and, although the grip of the two thugs stayed strong, they gave her enough leeway to twist and look at the boss behind the desk.

She blew her hair from her face. "Evander Manzani..." Known as Vex on the street. Even saying his name tightened her chest. "I come here because he can't get in. Him and his people. They can't... get to me here."

His head bobbed in a simple backward nod. The thugs let her go and McDade's lazy hand moved in a single finger point toward the rug. She touched her cleavage and there was another subtle nod. Straightening her dress, she tried to be graceful about sweeping her purse from the floor in her return to her previous spot on the stag head.

"You want McDade protection," he stated like it was fact.

"No," she said, adamant in gesture and gaze. "I am absolutely not asking for McDade protection." Because, for one thing, it came with a price. "This is not a serious... It's stupid. It's childish..." The slight descent of his brow sparked a frantic shot of fiery panic inside her. "No, not... Not you. You're not..." Babbling? Was she babbling? What the hell was wrong with her? Inhaling, she held the breath and then let it go. "Look, Evander Manzani is a child. A thirty-four-year-old child. We have history. Ridiculous history. I'm the toy he never got to play with. That's all this is. It is not a part of your war, a part of your... whatever. I got sick of them showing up at my place, sick of his stupid games. I came here because I was left alone."

"You get hit on every night."

Several times and it unnerved that someone on his crew noticed. "That I can deal with," she said. "Evander Manzani is two bullets short of a full clip, okay? Something, someday, eventually, will make him snap. I may not be involved in his world, your world, but I know enough about it not to want any part of it. Right now, he thinks it's a game. One day, he'll get tired of that game."

"And take what he wants?"

"Even he wouldn't be that stupid," she muttered, though sometimes wondered if arrogance outweighed good sense with him.

Did Evander actually have any of the latter in the first place? Unlikely.

Salving her lower lip, her teeth found it as her eyes drifted to the view of the dance floor beyond the windows.

"You don't think your father would stop him?" Her focus flashed to Ire. "I'm flattered. You chose a McDade over your own kin… You lack integrity, trust, but your survival instinct is strong… it drives you."

"I thought you didn't know who I was."

This time his smile was much more apparent though sly in a chilling, sinister way that brought those prickles back to her flesh.

"Did I say that, Miss McLeod?"

No. Now that he mentioned it, he hadn't said that. "If you knew who I was, why did you ask? A test?"

"That you failed, cailín," he said, rising to go to a decanter in the corner.

"Because I didn't tell you my name? It's Sersha, not Colleen."

Though the word did sound good rolling off his Irish tongue like that. Everything probably did.

He looked out over the club below. "Vex is obsessed with you. Has been for years." Yes, though she got intermittent reprieves from his infatuation when something, or someone, else caught his eye. For some reason, it always came back to her. And this most recent fixation was more intense than usual. "Do you want it?"

"Do I want what?"

He poured three fingers of whatever was in the decanter. Whiskey of some kind, she'd bet. Irish, no doubt.

"His attention," he said, replacing the stopper and lifting the glass. "Do you use it to your advantage?"

He sipped the liquor. Instead of returning to his seat, he passed the desk to come toward her.

"I don't know what that means," she said when he stopped less than a foot in front of her. "You think I'm playing with him? With this feud between your families?"

"Pieces have moved recently," he said. "The board has changed."

"I'll say." In more ways than one. "If you know who I am, who my father is, my grandfather, you know I'm aware of that."

"I know who your brother is too."

"Don't do that," she said, trying not to sneer at him as she shook her head. "Don't threaten my family like you're going to go out there and hurt them. If you wanted to hurt my brother, you'd have done it for a dozen other reasons, not because his sister sat at your bar a few nights."

"Why did you come to me?" he asked. "Why come to the McDades before your own family?"

On a blink, she forced her eyes to his. "I didn't come to you for protection, I already said that. If what I've heard about you is true, you're no idiot. You know what happens if I tell my brother, if I tell my grandfather about Evander. They're professionals and this is personal."

And because she didn't need them losing focus. She didn't want them hurt or going after people who wouldn't blink before pulling the trigger.

He sipped again. "Because you're the toy Vex never got to play with," he murmured.

Was she staring? His eyes *were* green. A darker green than she'd ever seen. Was it real? Maybe not. Could be contacts. In the low light, it was difficult to tell. He raised the glass to her. Was he…? Was she supposed to…?

With heat enveloping the dizziness in her head, she needed an anchor, or, at minimum, some relief. Taking the glass, she drank, probably more than she should have. It burned all the way down, but at least the sensation concentrated her focus.

She didn't see McDade turn his head until he spoke.

"Hock and Snuff."

The glass descended from her lips.

"Want Daly?" Curtain Guy asked.

"Yeah," McDade said, taking the glass and returning to his desk.

"Miss McLeod." And now she was Miss McLeod? Respect? That was Curtain Guy, gesturing at her, holding an arm toward the door. "Come this way."

McDade's concentration was on his phone. Good. She wanted to be forgotten. Better forgotten than in the basement. Though, that could've been a good story… if she'd made it out alive.

No, remember, one mafia family on her ass was enough.

THREE

THEY'RE STILL THERE.

Peeking through the living room blinds was supposed to put her mind at ease. They weren't supposed to still be there. McDade's thugs. Parked at the curb.

At being escorted from Stag the previous night, she'd expected the goons to toss her into the gutter. Instead, Curtain Guy poured her into the back of a decked-out Bentley with more expensive liquor in an apparently custom-made cubby.

She didn't touch it. She tried not to touch anything. Her head was still spinning when the car stopped outside her building.

How had they known where she lived? What else did they know? Dwelling on paranoia wouldn't end well. She went to bed sure the universe would've reset itself by morning.

Yet there she was, peeking out of her own blinds, looking at the car outside. Had they been there all night?

She had no choice except to go out. Steeple, her boss, was expecting her. Monday morning meant staff meeting. Steeple didn't need to know anymore than her father or brother. Vex would get over it. He always did eventually, until the next time rolled around.

Locking her apartment, she went downstairs, holding her head high. By the time she opened the communal door, a guy was propped against the car, arms folded. Tall, cute, and smiling in a dangerous, *"I could snap any second"* kind of way.

"Miss McLeod," he said, boosting off the front fender to open the rear door.

"What are you doing?" she asked, righting the strap of her purse on her arm. "Have you been out here all night?"

"No!" he said, smiling again. "The guys kept watch while I got some zees. You're in good hands, Miss McLeod."

"What is going on here?" she asked. "Are you stalking me?"

Like she didn't have enough trouble with that.

His smile vanished and he slammed the door to advance on her, getting up close. She held her ground. She always held her ground.

"You're under McDade protection, Miss McLeod. Me and my brothers are under orders to put ourselves between you and trouble. You keep that in mind. You've got the power to start a war. If you do, make sure it's one we can win, else you'll be the one paying for it too." His smile was slow, then he backed off to open the door and gestured inside again. "Miss McLeod."

Shit. Well, she wasn't going to wrestle him in the street. It was a ride to work. If she kept her nose clean, everything would be fine.

Stepping forward, she put a hand on the top of the door and paused to look over it at him.

"What's your name?"

"Daly," he said. "You have nothing to worry about, Miss McLeod. We're here to keep you safe."

She got in and the door closed. Had she just leaped from the frying pan to the fire?

The drive to work wasn't long. Tempting as the beckoning liquor was, it was maybe a little extreme to go into work lubed. Especially on a Monday morning. What would that mean for the rest of the week?

Daly was there to open her door before she'd even grabbed her purse. Was she living in a parallel universe? Suddenly she felt like a trophy wife on her way to the spa.

Daly closed the door behind her.

When he turned, she was right there waiting. "Are you going to follow me everywhere?"

"Yeah," he said without shame or apology.

"You don't have to. I'm fine. There's no reason to—"

"Miss McLeod, you can talk to me and my guys as much as you want, but you don't give the orders."

"What does that mean?"

"Means talk don't mean nothing. Unless it comes from Ire."

Ire… "That's what they call Connel McDade," she said, which was stupid because, of course, Daly knew that.

"Aye," he said. "From the top to the bottom."

"But he is the top," she said. "Wasn't his father murdered?"

"Coupla decades ago."

"On the order of Ire's uncle, right? Burl McDade?"

"Wanna know about the boss? Ask the boss," he said and looked at the building next to them. "We going in?"

"I'm going in. You won't get past security."

A sinister light sprang to his eye. "Bet you lunch I will."

And if she didn't make sure of that, there could be a scene. This was her life now.

Security wasn't exactly a high priority in the Collier Communications building. The Chronicler was just one of many CollCom divisions and subsidiaries housed in the Midwest HQ.

Far as she could tell, the guard by the front desk was more for show than anything else. Somewhere in the building was a security office; she'd seen their number in the directory. Despite the rent-a-cops, they got to the elevator and up to her floor without any issues. Great, this Daly guy was going to think she was full of it.

Even their usual guy, Paolo, wasn't in his booth on their floor. Typical.

Thoughts of humiliation quickly disappeared when she saw the massive floral arrangement sticking up from behind the reception desk hutch.

Lucy leaped to her feet. "Sersha!"

"Morning," she said, ignoring Daly loitering behind her. "What's going on?"

The receptionist lifted the vase to the higher level of the desk. "For you!" She didn't even take the card. "Your secret admirer… Again…! Aren't you curious who it is?" She knew who it was, just didn't reveal his identity to the masses. "It's so exciting. He's clearly mad about you."

"He's mad, I'll give you that," she said, stepping backward, right into Daly, so he got a sharp elbow in the ribs. "That's for sure."

"Do you want them on your desk?"

"Do I ever want them on my desk?"

Lucy's light faded. "No… I don't know why you're not stoked about this. It's so romantic."

Not in her opinion. Sending flowers to her work was cliche. Bad movie material. Evander Manzani would never sweep her off her feet, that was for sure. But for any guy to have a chance, he'd need to do more than open an account with a florist. Talk about by rote. Flowers told her nothing about the man or sent any message that might entice her.

Romance wasn't dead, it just looked different than it used to.

Most everyone was present when she got to Steeple's office. The editor was easy-going; he trusted his people. She couldn't remember the last time everyone under his purview made it to the Monday morning meeting. One or more of them was usually caught up in some story that diverted them from routine. Lucky their boss didn't crack any whip given she was bringing criminals into their peace.

Trying to slip in without disturbing the flow of the meeting, Daly prevented her from closing the door by wedging himself in the space.

"What are you doing?" she hissed, fighting against the boot he had planted against the door. "You can't come in here."

"Ire tell me that?"

"Jesus," she whispered, aware her colleagues would drink in every detail. "This is a room full of reporters. You can't be in here. Discussions are confidential."

Technically, all of Steeple's reporters were investigative. Each tended to have a niche, but given the right story and enough faith, Steeple allowed a lot of latitude.

"Won't I read it in the paper tomorrow?"

"No," she said. "These meetings are private."

Though her life was becoming more public by the second.

His ease cooled. "There are two ways to do this, Miss McLeod."

And his expression said he'd be okay with the hard way too. So she wasn't going to her meeting… but she would be going back to Stag that night. No way this could continue. Ire had to call his people off. They wouldn't take the order from her, but they would from the man at the top.

FOUR

DALY DIDN'T ASK questions when she came down from her apartment in a hunter-green bateau-neck cocktail dress at eleven p.m. Much later than she would usually go to Stag. With the McDades on her curb, the Manzanis would hang back. She guessed anyway. Maybe after a month of her not being home, they'd given up.

Though the flowers at the office suggested Evander wasn't completely over it yet.

Daly opened the back door of the Bentley and closed it once she was inside.

Her day had been surreal. After skipping the meeting, she sat at her desk with Daly loitering nearby the whole time. That meant she couldn't fill Steeple in about what the hell was going on even after the meeting was done. So she sent a vague email and put a story together using the police dailies and interviews by phone. Not her favorite way to do her job.

She shouldn't be mad. The McDades were protecting her… weren't they? It felt like control. Was a family like the McDades capable of altruism? No.

Perhaps. They weren't her area of expertise… yet. So much about them was myth and with what happened recently… Was it anger that churned up inside her? Maybe. But the questions were driving her crazy. She needed to know. She needed to ask. To get answers. Not knowing drove her nutty.

According to Daly's tight lips, the only way she'd get answers was to go to the top. And that was exactly her intention. Not that she'd told her bodyguard.

No, she waited until they arrived at the club and he'd let her out of the car onto the sidewalk. It helped that he opened one arm to her and the other to the VIP entryway. No more lining up behind a rope. No more tickets or metal detectors. The zip of a thrill at her new status may have bedded deeper if it wasn't for her determination.

Security stepped aside, and she went in. After a few feet, she stopped. At the curtain over the stairway. The two security guards didn't move; they kind of peeked at her and then each other. Well, if she wasn't always surprising McDade muscle.

"I want to see him." Both guys in front looked over her head. Daly. She spun on the spot to address him. "I want to see him."

"Alotta people do."

"You told me Ire was the only way."

For a second, he said nothing. Was he going to give? It wasn't like she could fight her way past the hulks behind her. Daly gave the guards the nod.

When she turned again, security stepped aside to let her ascend the enclosed staircase. That it was only maybe four feet wide would've been fine if it wasn't for the goons loitering at regular intervals, sucking in all the oxygen.

Adrenaline crept in as her heart sped up and she climbed higher. With thirty or so stairs, this Ire really did lord over his empire. The door at the top of the stairs didn't open for her as it had the previous night.

Without even thinking about what she wanted to say, she turned that handle and strode inside.

"I don't know who the hell gave you permission—"

Three men in suits sat at the desk with Ire McDade. Obviously, he was in the position of power; solo, dominating his side of the desk. As for the trio opposite him? The two naked blonde women kissing and groping each other on the chesterfield distracted her from scrutinizing them.

Naked. The bare beauties caressed each other like lovers completely alone in their intimacy.

"Men," the Irish overlord said, "you know Miss McLeod."

It took a second to drag her focus back to Ire. The other guys were glancing back and forth. Frowning. All but one of them anyway.

That guy stared. Gawped. "Wait, she's…"

"McLeod?"

"She's the…"

"Police Superintendent's daughter," another of the guys said.

That guy was familiar. In fact, she'd say they all were.

"Said your piece?" Daly asked from behind her.

So she hadn't come up alone. The curtain in the corner moved and Curtain Guy appeared again, pausing when he noticed her.

"Problem, Ire?" Curtain Guy asked.

"No problem," Ire replied.

One guy at the desk laughed. "Shit, Ire, is there a family you don't control with sex in this town?" He slapped a hand on the desk to push himself to his feet. "If you'd told us you were boning the old man's youngest, we'd have shaken hands the minute we walked in."

Ire stood as the man offered his hand. The others at the table followed.

"Stakes stay the same," Ire said, shaking one hand, then the next.

"Five percent," another guy said, but her focus remained on the first.

"You're Sylvester Babcock," she said, pointing at him. Daly took her shoulders to ease her aside. "You work on the City Council with my grandfather."

The men approached.

"I won't tell if you won't," Babcock said and winked as he passed.

Winking? Since when did her grandfather's friends get so sleazy?

"Daly," Ire said, and the hands left her shoulders.

When she glanced back, her guard was filtering out after the posse of city officials. Older men in cheap suits, she should've figured them out sooner.

"Niall."

Ire again.

"Aye?" Curtain Guy asked, also known as Niall apparently.

"Aye," Ire replied.

What the hell was going on?

Niall clucked his tongue twice and the blondes disengaged to leap up and scurry to him. He took two capes from hooks by the door and handed them over as the women disappeared down the stairs.

"Aye?" Niall asked again, looking only at the boss sauntering around the desk.

"Aye," Ire said once more.

Without another word, Niall went down the stairs, closing the door behind him.

They were alone. With all the coming and going, maybe she should've done the math sooner.

They were alone.

Alone.

"What is that?" she asked, taking a single step. "What is aye?"

"Means yes."

"I know what it means," she said, almost sneering at him. "What were you saying yes to?"

"You came in with something on your mind, cailín," he said, propping himself on the front of the desk, folding his arms.

"My name's Sersha."

"I know your name."

"But you get it wrong… on purpose," she said. "Why would you do that?"

"Never been one for following rules," he said, leaving his perch to round it again, going to the decanter in the corner.

Yeah, but there were rules and there was rude. Why would a guy like him care either way? More to the point, why did she care so much? Because of the tingle at the base of her spine and the shiver across her shoulder blades. She liked it. Damn her, but she did. Liked the rumble of his words, how they vibrated and rasped her most sensitive spots without him so much as looking her way.

This was a bad guy. Bad. Worse even than Evander Manzani. Evander still ran around with a gang of buddies, acting out while his father did the real work of the family.

Ire McDade didn't answer to a father. He was a law unto himself.

"Why were those guys here? The City Hall guys?" she asked. "That other one. Onslow. He works under the City Clerk."

"Aye," he said, turning as he raised the heavy crystal tumbler to his lips. "He does."

"Why would you have them here?"

"Calm nerves."

"Calm their nerves? Why would coming here to…" His dark eyes locked on hers, the glass stayed at his mouth, but he wasn't drinking. "You wanted them to see me. You used me."

"Like you used me."

"I did not—"

"Why'd you come to this club every night for a month?"

"That wasn't using you," she said, marching onto the rug. "Your club is here. It's open to the public. I'm the public. I didn't ask anything of you—"

"Has my boy not looked after you all day?"

"No," she asserted, approaching the desk to put her clutch down. "Your '*boy*' has followed me everywhere all day. I was afraid to go to the restroom in case he followed me there too. I can't do my job with him looking over my shoulder all the time."

"You're in one piece, are you?" he said, strolling closer.

"Why the hell do you do that? How are you just so calm and…? You can't imprison a woman and not expect her to be upset."

Licking his lips, he nodded in the door's direction. "Walk out," he said, mesmerizing her with his gaze. "You're no one's prisoner, cailín."

"That's not my name," she said, heavy heat crowding her belly when he stopped in front of her.

Her mouth watered. Something was wrong. It felt like ants were trailing up her spine to the back of her neck. The side of her leg touched the desk. Nothing was behind her, no trap, no fence or wall. Yet, as she slid along the hard edge of the solid desk, he moved with her like she'd asked for something. She hadn't. Shouldn't. Yet…

"Drink?" he said, offering the glass.

The moment it was in her palm, he swept her hair from her shoulder. She tossed her head back to gulp the potent whiskey. Was she aware of him stooping over her? Maybe. Yes. She was. And didn't resist or object. Curiosity won out. When his lips grazed the side of her neck, her eyelids sank. The contact was… so delicate, yet… There was power. She shouldn't be drugged by it, shouldn't let him take the empty glass from her hand to put it on the desk she boosted herself onto.

Damn, she'd done it. Of her own freewill, she parted her thighs to accept him between them. As she responded to the heat of his kiss on her jaw, she turned her head, his rose and then their mouths were…

Oh, God, he tasted like her, like them, the burning liquid flavored his tongue, intoxicating her as the liquor had. Except this drug was all natural. Biology. Of need. Of want. Of primal urge to…

His palm skimmed under her skirt, up over her hip to the band of elastic resting there. It wasn't right. She shouldn't plant her hands on the desk behind her and raise her ass to let him slide her panties down her legs.

Not only did she do exactly that, but when he stepped back, she kicked the silk away and snatched the back of his neck to yank his mouth to hers again, demanding its attention. She didn't want to be without it. Not yet. Not now. Addicted to the heat of his forceful tongue, she needed to battle back, to push with the same strength, to give him the same assurance that seared her.

As she shoved the jacket from his shoulders, his hands went under her skirt to pull her ass to the edge of the desk, forcing her against the thick column of his own want. Shit. She wanted it. Wanted him. Clutching at the back of his head, she couldn't have him close enough. Why hadn't they done this the previous night? Why weren't they doing this every damn minute of the day?

Tendrils of cool air on her spine proceeded the rasp of her dress zipper. With no warning, he slammed her down, knocking the wind out of her. The creep of his sly smile might have been sinister if it wasn't for the glaze in his alight gaze. Whatever chemistry was at work between them, he was hooked too.

In that second, it wasn't possible to say no. Instinct moved her as he wanted her to move, under his spell, his control, his authority. Sliding the dress from her shoulders down to uncover her breasts, he was quick to snatch her hips and jerk her to the edge again.

He bowed, unbuckling his belt, his lips finding hers as her legs wound around him. A mew of need escaped her throat. It was too fast and too slow. She wanted to be complete. That would only happen if he got his goddamn cock out his pants faster and—

"Ire!"

A masculine shout came from the corner. The man on top of her twisted and there was a shot. A gunshot. A scream. Whose scream?

Still panting, it took a second to register the anger on the profile of the man locked in the embrace of her legs.

"Shit, Dingo, what the fuck did you…?"

That was a third voice. Niall, maybe.

"Get him the fuck out of here before I finish him," the guy above her snarled, his accent thick.

The startling venom in those words brought her to her elbows. Dazed by endorphins, the view was almost unbelievable. Niall was there, with two others, picking up an unknown guy. Blood. There was blood all over the front of the stranger's shirt. He was injured. Shot. Her mouth opened slow. Someone put a bullet in him, and Ire was the only man holding a gun.

FIVE

THE STARTLING CLUNK of a weapon hitting the desk came at the same time her legs were pushed down and her hand grabbed. They were moving. Where were they…? The bleeding guy and those helping him went down the stairs. Her playmate led her the other way, through the curtain in the corner into a small square hall. Stairs up and a door next to them.

Up was their route. Where were they going? What was…? At the top of the stairs, he doubled back, rounding the hip-high wall separating the stairs from the floor. It was a living room. Was it?

She didn't take much of it in before they passed through an open section in the wall. A bedroom. Oh, she knew what that was.

The gun in his other hand caught the light as he tossed it to the floor by the end of the low-profile bed.

"You shot that guy," she said as he took her waist to pull her in front of him, the bed at her back. "Why did you do that?"

"He interrupted," he said, hooking an arm around her to drag her zipper down the rest of the way.

Her dress fell to the floor. "You shot him. That's…" A complete overreaction? Alone in the shadowy space, it wouldn't be wise to say that out loud. "You shot him in front of the Police Superintendent's daughter."

Probably not smart to remind him of that either.

"Aye," he said, unbuttoning his shirt. "Now you have leverage."

"Leverage…"

When his shirt went so did her concerns. It wasn't like she was a stranger to attractive men. Healthy, fit, muscular men who had to spend half their life at the gym to look that good. At least this guy had reason. In his line of work, it probably paid to be fit. Who knew when he might next be running or fighting for his life?

Sweeping the hair back from her shoulders, he didn't ask before unhooking her bra and freeing her arms. "You're a beauty, cailín."

Drawn to the stag head silhouette tattooed high on his chest, just beneath his left clavicle, her fingertips rose to touch it. For a few seconds, she traced the shape. He didn't linger and dipped to suck the side of her neck, piercing her with a pleasurable pain that took her right back to where they'd been.

Snagging her hand, he guided it to his loose belt. He wanted this. She wanted this.

"This is a bad idea," she said, loosening his fly. "We shouldn't do this." He squeezed her breast, tweaking the tip and massaging her with his palm while trailing his lips up to her jaw again. Though her mouth was tempted toward his, she found enough strength to lay a hand over that tattoo and push him back to meet his eye. "You're dangerous."

"Taste's good, doesn't it?" he murmured, seizing her hips to toss her to the middle of the bed.

She was naked. How did that happen? How did she get herself there? And, shit, he was right. Being with him tasted better than anything that had ever passed her lips. Stroking the black silk sheets, she watched him strip down and crawl onto the bed, continuing over her until she was flat on her back beneath him.

"We have to use protection," she said, her fingertips trailing down his torso.

He reached for her ear. Like a magic trick, instead of a quarter, he produced a condom from nowhere. As his mouth sank onto hers again, her lips curled. She had to cut herself some slack. So what if she was attracted to him? He obviously returned the interest. Nothing wrong with two adult, consenting people—

Pain. Shit. He was trying to push into her. Relax. Fuck. On the next attempted advance, she gasped and shoved him back, digging her nails into his shoulder. The darkness in his eyes ensnared her.

She panted through the ache. "I've heard about McDade men."

"All true," he said, dipping to kiss her cheek and her chin, tasting his way to her breasts and lower, all the way to the hot pool of desire between her thighs.

She hissed an inhale when he sucked her clit and flickered it with his tongue. Shit, the guy knew what he was doing. Had she ever thought he wouldn't pleasure a woman? The sweet slip of his certain tongue through her folds was better than anything her fingers or any toy had achieved.

Her hands sank into his hair as he sunk his kiss into her. "Shit," she whispered, her knees rising, parting further. "Goddamn that's good. God… oh, Conn." His pampering stopped. The interruption brought her head from the bed. And there he was, looking up the length of her, through her cleavage, right into her eyes. Fuck. She'd never known danger lived and breathed in her city… or that it was so damn exhilarating. "I want you inside me…" The words came out in one long rush of breath. "I don't give a fuck if it hurts." He surged up over her again. "Do it. Hard and fast. Hurt me."

His lips went to one side though he ducked to swipe them across hers one last time before bracing himself on an arm and thrusting into her.

God-fucking-hell! It did hurt. Enough to water her eyes and tighten her chest. Fuck, searing fucking—he was in, all the way, filling her fuller than she'd ever been filled. And the pain became pure, hot pleasure.

She lost track of time, of his thrusts, of everything as pressure built within her.

"Connel," she moaned his name, digging her nails into his bicep. "Please… Oh, damnit, please…"

Who the hell knew what she was begging for? For it to be over? For the indulgence to reach its apex and consume her? For the moment, her experience with him, to go on and on and never end? Could they die right there? How was it possible to live after experiencing such pleasure?

Her eyes were closed until he surged forward, tilting his pelvis, slamming it against her, then, he stopped. Completely stopped. Almost completely… His hips undulated, arousing her clit with his body. Mmm, how was he doing that? She hadn't known it was possible. For a guy to be so deep inside her and stimulating her that way at the same time.

"Connel," she whispered, planting her hands on his chest almost like she wanted to push him away.

Except her fingers curled until her nails bit into his flesh. She could feel it, knew she was hurting him, yet she didn't stop. He didn't ask her to, he leaned into it, staring down at her, almost daring her to dig deeper.

As the beat of her heart slowed and she caught her breath syncing to his, everything relaxed. Then, snap, he rolled them over, pulling her on top of him, right onto his cock again.

"Feel better?" he asked.

His entitled hand ascended her body, straightening her up to straddle him, before enjoying her breasts with both hands.

"Deeper," she whispered, squirming on him. "Shit, you feel so good. Fuck…"

With her fists balled low on his stomach, he kept playing with her breasts as she pushed herself up and sank onto him over and over, moving in every direction all at the same time. He made it impossible to be still. She was learning places inside of herself she hadn't known existed.

"That's it, baby." His voice came out as that low rumble he was oh so good at, thick with his arousing accent. "Good girl… Just like that. You are a good girl."

He felt good in that corner. Pushing that way, she rode him harder, letting his head hit her deep. Then he yanked her the other way and sat up, crushing her clit between them.

"Shit, Connel."

"That pretty little mouth," he murmured, hooking his arms beneath hers, around her shoulders, pulling her against him. "Your daddy know how dirty it gets in bed?"

"I reserve some things for the lucky few." She accepted his kiss as he slanted her back, balancing her weight on his forearms, increasing the pressure between their linked bodies. "Connel McDade…" Clenching her teeth, the pulse of lingering orgasm teetered so close it threatened to ruin her. "You don't finish me this second, I'm going to get that damn gun and force you to do it with your fucking talented tongue."

A deep, rough laugh left his lips as they sampled hers again. Continuing his theme of keeping her off-kilter, he shoved her onto her back and drove into her again a couple of times, delivering a climax so powerful that her lungs froze.

She couldn't take air in. Couldn't expel it or feel anything except the flood of hormones rushing through every inch of her, gathering in the clench of her inner muscles.

Heat. Satisfaction. Desperation. Every atom of her being was alive, taut in the frozen moment of delight.

Shit. He was good. Too good. More than any woman would be able to handle alone.

That wasn't the point.

They were sating a need. Satisfying a curiosity. Pleasing each other with what nature gave them.

It wasn't about tomorrow or what came next. It was about that moment. The hedonistic satisfaction of two people enticed by a potent magnetism so powerful it hadn't needed words. It went unsaid. Yet, they'd both let it take them over. Only time would tell if either of them would live to regret it.

SIX

"YOU'VE GOT ISSUES."

"You have no idea, Steeple," she said, sitting opposite her boss at his desk the next day. "No idea."

"What's with him?" he asked, looking toward the glass panels in his wall that showcased the bullpen beyond.

More specifically, to the guy standing guard, blocking the panel by the door. That she'd kept him on the other side of it was a small mercy. One not to be taken for granted.

"That's Daly."

"Yeah, and according to my sources, he works for the McDades."

She laughed. "You sit behind your desk and leave all the hard work to us. What sources do you have?"

"You know the golden rule," he said, swinging left to right in his chair.

"I don't give up sources because mine are real. Yours are imaginary, less chance they'll get in trouble."

"I paid my dues for plenty of years. My sources haven't dried up yet," he said. "Am I wrong?"

"About Daly? No. He's on McDade payroll."

"And his interest in you?"

"Is this why you called me in here?" she asked. "To quiz me about Daly?"

"Are you avoiding the question?"

"Are you interrogating me?"

"Is this something to do with the flowers that show up three times a week?"

"Are you asking about my personal life?"

Everyone noticed. Of course their natures were to get to the bottom of mysteries. Her colleagues couldn't have missed the bouquets, but this was the first time Steeple asked her straight out.

Her boss wasn't confrontational. How many times had he reminded his reporters that honey often reaped more bees? This was less interrogation and more curious sparring. Still, she wasn't sure Steeple was ready to hear the truth. Or that she was ready to tell it.

"That what the McDades are to you?" he asked. "Personal?"

"Steeple," she said, warning him his teasing was growing old.

"Okay. Okay," he said, laughing as he pushed back in his chair. "You ruin all my fun."

He didn't know how close he was to a raw nerve.

"What did you need me for?" she asked.

"I don't need you, I… How close are you and Immie these days?"

"Imogen?" she asked. "Stratford? Imogen Stratford?"

"Yeah," he said.

"Because of her relationship with Lachlan?"

"Yeah, she was with your brother for years," he said. "Do you hang out?"

She frowned. "Why? What's going on?"

"Nothing…" He sealed his lips and puffed out his cheeks. "She's got a wild theory about something… kind of in your field."

"You want me to talk to her about it? What field are we talking?"

"Nothing. Forget it."

"If I ask Lach, will he tell me?" she asked, though it was kind of a hollow threat.

Given her recent life developments, and surprise connections, she was in no hurry to converse with her too-smart-for-his-own-good older brother.

"I don't know. If I ask him about Daly, will he tell me what's going on there?"

"You're going to call my brother?" she asked not believing he would. "You're not going to call him. What's this about?"

"You know I think you're great," Steeple said, linking his fingers when he sat up to lay his forearms on the desk. "I'd print every word you ever wrote…"

"If this is about my article yesterday—"

"This is about you not following up on your exposé. You worked for months gaining the confidence of people in the Manzani network. The family, your insights… you know it got national recognition." Yeah, and reignited Evander's interest in her. Hence her residency at Stag. "You could've had a series of them. Could've gone deeper. With your connection to law enforcement and your penetration of organized crime… Why do I feel like you stopped listening?"

Because she wasn't the one doing the penetrating last night. And damn if she couldn't stop thinking about it.

He'd got up and left her the minute he climaxed. Connel. Ire. He'd gone into a closet and reappeared from what she thought was a bathroom, fully clothed, without so much as looking at her before returning to his office.

Not only would it have been rude to loiter, she also didn't want to clash with whoever might come next. Ire McDade was a virile guy. He'd gone from the blondes to her to… whoever he next made a move on.

"Sersha, hello?" Steeple asked, waving at her. "Are you okay?"

"Yeah, yeah," she said, fighting to push the flashbacks aside.

"I've gotta say, when I heard a McDade was following you around… Are they next? Are you switching your focus? Going deeper into McDade territory?"

Oh, way further than he knew. "I hear you," she said, pouncing to the front of her seat then to her feet. "Let me think about it."

"Ser—"

"I'll do it right," she said, "not for the sake of it. Let me make some calls."

Wasn't she supposed to be getting the Manzanis out of her life? Yeah, she could maybe write about the McDades, but who hadn't? Since the trial and the testimony… It had died down. Maybe that was the right time to take a look at the family from a different perspective.

Shit. Talk about unethical. She couldn't screw a guy then decide to write about him the next day. Could she? Who would she rather write about, the Manzanis or the McDades?

This may not end well for any of them.

SEVEN

"I TOLD YOU TO CALL, SCAMP."

"I know," she said, ducking under Strat's arm to head into his apartment without express permission. "You wouldn't believe what I had to go through to get here, Strat."

Passing his kitchen, she shed her jacket on her way into the living room.

"What did you do?" he asked, that edge of suspicion in his damn knowing voice.

Few people would understand her relationship with Kurt Stratford, also known as just Strat. Their friendship was sort of a secret. A source was one label she could put on him, but it was more than that. The guy was closer to her dad's age than hers. Still, for them, for her, it worked.

His daughter, Imogen, was a reporter at The Chronicler too. Maybe that was something to do with why they connected. Could be, but she was no psych major and chose instead just to appreciate the man and his acceptance.

"Not going to offer me some coffee?" she asked.

"Ser…"

"I want to go back to the beginning," she said, dropping into the armchair by the window. "I want to hear more about your relationship with Silvio Manzani."

Evander's father. Writing about the patriarch of the Manzanis may be safer than pursuing the progeny obsessed with stalking her.

"You know, women these days…" Strat said, sauntering over to sit in his recliner. "None of you know what's good for you."

"Is that right?"

His apartment wasn't huge. The bedroom door was between their chairs and the couch shared a wall with the TV affixed above it.

"Like my Immie, always got something to prove."

Yeah, and it did occur to her to ask if father knew what his daughter was into. But just because Steeple knew Imogen was into something didn't mean Strat did.

"You adore your daughter."

"I do. But she doesn't know what's good for her and neither do you," he said. "You don't want to get into Silvio's business. Deeper into his business. You're lucky you got away clean last time."

"Clean?" she asked. "You think I got away clean?"

Sometimes Strat was the only one holding her up. So what if he was old enough to be her father? He was the only one she could be completely honest with… almost completely.

"I think your exposé strolled dangerously close to defamation."

"It didn't cross any lines," she said, dumping her purse on the floor. "We have a team of lawyers paid to cover our asses on that score."

"You think the Manzanis care about that?" he asked. "The law is the least of your worries, Scamp."

"They couldn't publicly come after me."

"Because of your brother? Your father? Grandfather? If the McLeod men could dismantle the power of organized crime in this city, they'd have done it already."

"Are we getting into this debate again?" she asked, slipping off her shoes to tuck her feet up on the chair.

As she settled back, she glanced at the nearby blinds. Had Daly found her yet?

"If you're settling in for the night, I'll order pizza…" Strat said. "Don't you have a family of your own?"

"A workaholic family."

He laughed and got up to go into the kitchen. "Calling me a deadbeat?"

"If your daughter keeps the same hours I do, she's on call twenty-four seven."

"I was always more interested in you keeping hours with my son."

"Ah, another familiar topic. I don't even know Ford," she said, recognizing Strat's teasing smile as he approached with two beers to hand one over. "I know him, but I don't know, know him."

If anyone should have a relationship, it should be her and Imogen, given the woman also dated Lachlan for years. Somehow, they hadn't got it together as girlfriends, but she could hang out with Strat for hours and still be loathed to go home.

"Ford wouldn't be able to handle you," Strat said, settling in his chair again. "He's all about the straight and narrow."

"These days," she said, amused. "These days he's all about the straight and narrow. He hasn't always been that way. Weren't him and Dunn big on the underground fighting circuit? Chopping cars was their day job, but there's a rumor…"

Myth? Legend? The city's worst kept secret in certain circles.

"Yeah," he said, sinking into his lounger again.

"You know your son learned his mischievous ways from you."

"Yeah, thank God Bette took Immie."

"You both made that choice though, right? Imogen went to live with her mom, and Ford stayed in the city with you."

"Yeah, for all the good it did. We subjected Immie to enough scum and shady dealings when she was here on visits to scare her off for life. How come you think she was with the cop for so long? She wants a good guy."

"They say women go for men like their fathers."

"Bullshit," he said. "It's bullshit. Imogen wants a shining white knight hero. I couldn't be further from that. Who the fuck have I ever saved?" He tipped his bottle toward her. "And the guys in your family are all good and righteous, living their virtuous lives, but you're all about the bad boys. 'Bout as far away from your pop as you could get… Why'd you think you spend so much time in the gutter with me?"

"This isn't the gutter," she said, glancing around. "I like your place."

"And wading in with the Manzanis?" he asked. "Maybe Vex is exactly what you need, Scamp. You're drawn to the dark side."

"Dark is a better story."

"Yeah," he said, snickering as he swilled his beer. "The story's what you want."

"Don't laugh like that," she said, though her smile wasn't too distant. "Why else would I pursue these families and their stories?"

"Oh, come on," he said, reclining his chair. "You're talking to one of the original bad boys. You think I don't know what gets women like you off?" Her mouth opened in mock offense. He laughed again. "Hell, I lived on a steady diet of pussy just like yours for decades. Guys like me, the rough, dark, dangerous guys? We can sniff it out and know exactly how to get what we want without giving a shit if we hurt you."

"Evander obviously missed that memo. Or you're wrong about me."

"You need a man, Scamp. Vex is not man enough for you." Funny, she'd recently said the same thing… close to it anyway. "Growing up with your family… there's pressure on the good just like the bad."

"I could never live up to my father's expectations."

"Because you don't have a dick."

"Pretty much," she said, drinking some beer.

"Your daddy's bold… probably just as ruthless as Silvio Manzani or Burl McDade."

Burl McDade was Ire's uncle. Ire's incarcerated uncle.

"We haven't talked much about the McDades in prison."

"You wanted to talk about the Manzanis," he said. "The two families used to be close, you know, the McDades and Manzanis… Way back when the Byrnes and Dohertys were still a feature. They're all but gone now… Since the McDades took over what was left of the Dohertys' east coast division, the Midwest families have felt the power shift. And with the Gambattos falling apart, the McDades are grabbing all kinds of opportunities."

"You talk like it's some legit corporate empire."

"Maybe not legit, but it's more corporate now than the old days."

"Aww, your misspent youth."

"Damn right," he said. "You kids don't know what you've got."

"Thought you were lily white these days."

Rocking in his chair, he winked at her. "And that's what we say when anyone asks."

She laughed. "It's always double standards with guys like you."

"Guys like me fascinate you, baby. If you're looking for another story, be careful going too deep with the Manzanis."

"Why?"

"'Cause you're treading a line with that family. If you don't tip Vex over the edge, you'll get all kinds of the wrong attention from Silvio. You've gotta look after yourself."

"You don't like Evander," she said. "Him and Ford were friends once."

"They ran in the same circles, with the same crew, wouldn't call 'em friends. Vex was all about taking what he could get."

"He hasn't changed much."

"You want a story…?"

Intriguing. "Isn't that why I come to you? You always deliver, Strat."

"Think about going back in time… Maybe if you don't stray too close to the present, the Manzanis won't feel threatened."

Men like those in the Manzani family didn't feel threatened; they were too arrogant for that. Until the moment it was too late anyway. Just ask Burl McDade.

"Go on," she said, never one to refuse information.

"You wanna take a shot at solving a mystery?"

"A mystery?" she asked, buzzing with interest. "Tell me more."

Something to focus on. Something to sink her teeth into. Something other than memories of her lapse in judgment. She'd walked into Ire's office ready to demand he back off. Somehow, she'd ended up in his bed. It wouldn't happen again.

It wouldn't.

Would it?

EIGHT

WHEN SHE WALKED around the corner onto her street, she expected the Bentley to be parked outside her building and wasn't disappointed. Daly leaned against the side, arms and ankles crossed, watching her approach.

"Having a good night?" she called to him, swinging her purse at her side.

"You left your phone at work."

"I have experience slipping the net," she said, stopping in front of him. "Don't feel bad."

When she spun on the spot, intending to go inside, he grabbed her arm to whip her back around. "You think you can screw with us?"

Yanking her arm only tightened his grip. "Take your hands off me," she hissed.

"He'll put a choke chain on you so tight, you'll beg for every breath," he snarled, bowing to get his face closer to hers. "McDades protect what belongs to them. You belong to us now. You belong to him."

"Want to bet?"

He exhaled and jerked her aside to open the car's back door. "Let's see what Ire says."

"Who the hell do you think you—"

Daly slung her around, literally throwing her into the backseat. She immediately grabbed for the opposite door handle, but it wouldn't give. The door slammed behind her. Desperation brought her around fast, but all the tugging and pulling in the world wouldn't loosen the locks.

The car started moving so fast it pushed her back in the seat.

Shit. No points for guessing where they were going.

Okay, so she'd ditched the McDade posse. Hadn't she told Daly that she didn't want him following her everywhere? Yeah, but she'd failed to mention that to his boss while getting down and dirty with him. Suddenly, it didn't seem so necessary to avoid the liquor. She yanked the bottle from its slot and the stopper from the top. Who cared about being ladylike on the way to God knew what fate?

When they eventually stopped outside the club, the privacy screen buzzed halfway down. Trying the doors for escape would be too telling, so she didn't bother.

"Are you gonna cause trouble?" came Daly's voice from the front.

Options. What were her options? Patrons in the Stag line wouldn't help even if she screamed bloody murder. Anyone from the city knew who the club belonged to. Probably anyone from the state. Any tourist in the wrong place, wrong time who might think to be gallant would either get shot or put straight fast.

Ire shot a man just for interrupting an intimate moment. Anyone interfering in business probably got the basement treatment.

Even a good Samaritan calling the cops on the sly wouldn't work out for her. How would she explain being there to her dad and brother?

Daly was embarrassed, right? That was the root of his vicious mood. His boss couldn't be that mad... could he?

"McLeod?" Apparently, she was no longer a Miss. "Are you gonna cause trouble?"

"No," she said to Daly. "What good would that do?"

"Good," he said. "You learn fast."

As the screen buzzed up, doors opened.

She wasn't afraid. Wary was probably a better word. Loyalty between her and Ire didn't exist.

Her door opened and she waited until Daly bent to look inside before sliding to the edge of the seat and getting out.

He didn't *need* to touch her but grabbed her arm anyway, holding her close as he directed her inside and up the stairs.

She and Ire may be strangers, but there was something innate between them. They communicated through chemistry rather than words. Or was that her imagination?

Maybe that belief explained her lack of concern at being dragged into the boss's office again.

"This is becoming habit," she said more to herself than anyone else.

Ire sat behind his desk. On the far side, a laptop preoccupied Niall. Two guys sat at opposite ends of the Chesterfield. As the men's attention tracked to her, Daly closed in at her back.

"Did we insult you?"

Again with the insult question, only this one came from the couch. Maybe it was the standard McDade introduction.

"She's playing a game," Ire said, his voice low and slow. "She hasn't realized yet that she's the prize."

"I am not playing a game," she said, taking a step forward. At least, she started to. Daly's hand landed on her shoulder to stop her. It was ridiculous. Her chin swung to the side. "You think they're afraid of me? You've got to keep me over here in case, what? I try to assassinate someone with my non-existent ninja skills?" Opening her arms, she turned on the spot to face him. "You think I have a weapon? Frisk me."

"Boss'll do that later," came a masculine voice before a snicker that spread to the guys on the couch.

Niall couldn't think she wouldn't know he'd been the speaker. Not with an accent like that. Still, at least she didn't have to wonder whether her interlude with Ire was a secret. Apparently, he told his right-hand man, and their goons, everything.

Then she heard it.

That whimper.

That moan.

Like a woman lost in ecstasy… Like her…

Whirling around, she fixated on the sound. The laptop. Yes, she could feel every man's eyes on hers, but it was his, Ire's, that captured her focus.

"You asshole."

Was it just audio? Please, God, if she had any wish chips to cash—

Niall turned the laptop and there it was. Her. Them. In the bed upstairs, her on top, of course, his hands full with her breasts. Though that modesty didn't last.

Her eyes fixed on the screen. Ire hit the spacebar, pausing the image of her, head thrown back, sheer bliss on her face.

"Out," Ire said.

Daly retreated from behind her to open the door as the couch guys and Niall stood to head that way.

Her eyes met Ire's. Had this been his plan all along? Why hadn't she seen it coming? Had she believed a guy like him could be honest? Decent? Honorable?

The door closed, shutting them in. What did he expect her to do? Scream? Curse? Cry?

"This is simple," he said, opening a desk drawer to retrieve something. An envelope, that he tossed to the corner of the desk closest to her. "You're gonna take that to Babcock tomorrow."

Is that what he thought?

"Go screw yourself."

"Round two?"

"What kind of asshole films a woman without her consent?"

"Would you remember if I asked? You were sunk, baby." His hand hovered over the keyboard. "Need a reminder?"

Her feet moved before she thought. "It's illegal—"

"And?" That wasn't a deal-breaker in his house. He rose when she paused in front of the envelope. "All you have to do is go to his office and hand it over."

"You're insane," she spat, shaking with the anger that burned inside her. "If you think I'd ever do anything for—no. Forget it. I'm out of here."

Spinning around to stalk toward the door, she was done. God help any of the goons who might try to get in her way.

"That how your daddy feels?" he asked. She stopped. "Video like that gets out, your brother's career is over. Your grandfather, your father, both made it to Superintendent. Be a shame to dash Lachlan's hopes, so early…" She loathed turning, and from the look on his face, he knew it. "You told me not to threaten his life.

How about his career? His reputation? His dignity? You? The perfect McLeod princess, in my bed, screaming for a McDade. How will that go across with the superiors?"

Nausea sapped some of her anger. "You're a real asshole. The lowest kind of scum."

"There would be investigations into their past convictions," he said, enjoying each second of her torture. "Every decision. A few choice leaks would confirm just how intimate I've been with their cases."

"You haven't been intimate with—"

"People love a sex scandal."

And that was it. He had her and he knew it. Her respected family name would be dragged through the mud. Everything would be brought into question. Her attitude as a reporter. Her celebrated and praised exposé on the Manzanis would be slandered and dismissed. She'd be a joke. But that was nothing; that was deserved for her stupidity. Her family didn't deserve it.

Her grandfather loved the city he'd dedicated his life to serving. Growing older, he didn't talk about slowing down, but his career wouldn't have time to recover. What would he do but wither?

And her father. What about him? If he lost his job and the media hounded him as cases he'd overseen got reopened, he'd be ruined. His professional identity was what he valued most. Over his family, over everything else. Some part of him still wanted to earn his own father's esteem while he demanded it of his children.

And though it was her father's judgment that beat in the back of her head, it was her brother who squeezed her heart. Her brother was good. Better than any other man in the world. Pure of heart, honorable, filled with an unparalleled integrity that just wouldn't allow him to consider ever doing anything illicit.

What choice did she have?

"I do this and that's it," she said, marching over to snatch the envelope. "You destroy that recording and we're done. And get your guys to back off. I don't want them anywhere near me."

She didn't give him the chance to argue. Walking in there had not been her choice, and she resented the shit out of him for manipulating her. But this was it, a final act that would sever her life from the McDades forever.

NINE

DELIVER AN ENVELOPE. That wasn't difficult, was it? No. So why was she so nervous? She tried to tell herself it wasn't illegal. Could one of the country's strongest and most notorious crime bosses send someone on an errand that wasn't illegal? Instead of taking a bus or a cab, she walked the twelve blocks to City Hall.

Was she covering her tracks? Could she? Was he setting her up?

Daly and the McDade protectors hadn't been on her tail all day. What did that suggest? That he was respecting her wishes? Unlikely. Yet she couldn't test him, couldn't take the risk—

"Se—Sersha?"

Someone grabbed her arm.

She blinked around and took a second to process. "Dad," she said, clutching her purse closer. "Hi."

"What are you doing here?"

What was she doing there? Nothing she could tell her father. That meant thinking fast. "I haven't seen Grandpapa for weeks—"

"He's across town today," he said, frowning. "Giving a speech."

"Right," she said, though hadn't known that.

"I had a public safety meeting," he said, checking his watch. "Have you eaten?"

"No."

"No, because you never eat lunch," he said, taking her shoulder to turn her around. "Been the same since you were a kid. Come on, I'll buy you something."

This had to be Opposite Day. "You want to have lunch with me?"

"Sure," he said, taking his phone from his pocket. "I'll call Lach."

Of course he would. Because God forbid he spent any time alone with her. Lachlan, her brother, could be anywhere doing anything, and he'd come running. He responded to their father more like a superior officer than a parent. Just like he'd been raised.

Her brother was strong. Smart. Keener than her, sharper than their father, more likeable than their grandfather, he had it all. Yet, often, he was left explaining himself. It wasn't fair. He deserved a better family. She didn't know how he'd turned out so good when everything else was screwed up.

"He's on his way," her father said when he hung up and started walking. "We'll go to that Vyne restaurant you like."

Confused, her brow lowered. "I like? You mean the Italian place?" she asked and he nodded. "Imogen likes Vyne, Dad." Not that she didn't. "Lach's *ex*-girlfriend. You know they broke up, right?"

"It won't last. He'll fix it."

"How do you know he wants to?" she asked. "Sometimes relationships run their course."

"They've been together for years. They're going to get married."

That was startling enough that she almost stopped dead. "They're not engaged. When were they engaged? Did he ask you for Mom's ring?"

Also known as their grandmother's ring.

"No," he said. "But why wouldn't she want to marry him?"

"Dad, you better not say anything. Don't upset him."

"He doesn't get upset."

"Just because he doesn't show you doesn't mean he isn't upset. Please don't get on his case today."

"The two of you always stand in front of each other."

"Why shouldn't we?" Their mother died when she was young. With their father working all the time, Lachlan did more of the raising than the adult men in their family. "He takes too much on himself. You put too much on him."

"And this," he said in an annoyed snap. "You don't have to voice every thought in your head."

"It's my opinion," she said, aware distance was growing between them. "He won't say it."

"Does he say it to you?"

"No," she said. "But I—"

"Then you could be wrong. Your brother is strong. He was raised to be strong."

Shaking her head, he hadn't heard her at all. "Dad—"

"That's where your attention should be. Instead of getting yourself in trouble with the scum of the underworld, you should be looking for a strong partner. A man who will look after you."

"This is the twenty-first century. I take care of me."

"I lose sleep over it," he said like she hadn't spoken. "You out there without a husband. A real man. Someone strong. Someone with a clear head, smarts, bold. You need to think about the future."

"My biological clock isn't ticking yet," she said, pausing with him, waiting for the light to change. "I date men I'm attracted to…"

The moment the words came out, she wanted to grab them back. What the hell was she doing talking about her love life? Disagreeing with her father seemed rich when she wasn't exactly making the best choices of late.

"Which is exactly your problem. You make decisions based on your gut."

Her chin rose as they crossed the street. "Which is what you tell Lachlan to do all the time."

"That's different."

"Because he's male?"

"Because he has the McLeod instinct."

"And I have, what? Claiming not to be my father now?"

"Don't disrespect your mother." Just rolled off his tongue by rote. "You're addled like her. She never could focus on what was important."

"Amazing, look at that," she said, raising her wrist to check an imaginary watch. "Took you a whole two minutes to call me an idiot."

"You're too sensitive."

Something else he'd told her in the past. Frequently.

"It's not sensitivity," she said. "My point of view might—"

"Your brother's here already."

Beyond those on the sidewalk between them, her brother stood outside the restaurant up ahead. Wow, he didn't know how to disappoint.

He was smiling when they approached, though that gave way to concern as they got closer and his scrutiny narrowed.

"Didn't know you two needed a mediator," Lachlan said, bowing to kiss her head. "What's going on?"

"Just the usual," she said as he opened the door to hold it for her and their father.

"I thought you met at City Hall," Lachlan said as they sat in a booth.

"We did."

"And you rubbed each other the wrong way already? If only it was an Olympic sport."

"Let's order," her father said, passing out menus.

Another grab for control because he didn't want to talk about it.

No one spoke until the server came over to write their order.

Once the woman was gone, her brother inhaled. "So—"

"Oh," their father said, checking his phone. "I have to take this."

He slid out of the booth and went straight for the exit, raising the phone to his ear before the door closed behind him.

"What happened?" Lachlan asked. "He on your case?"

"About finding a man who'll look after me? Always. But it's more than that, he just… he doesn't like me."

"He loves you."

"You know, I used to think he loved mom too. But every quality I apparently share with her, he hates."

"You know what he's like."

"We have to make all these concessions for him and he makes none for us?"

"You should be used to it. He's never going to change."

"Again, so I'm supposed to?"

"You just have to accept it. Bet there are some things you don't like about me," he said, flashing her a grin. "You bitch to dad about those?"

"If I had the mental capacity, I would," she said, sinking back, running a hand through her hair. "Right now, you have to take a ticket."

"Need me to go big brother on anyone?"

His grin was gone, but she smiled, though exhaustion chased her. "I love you, Lach, but I can't imagine you being mean to anyone."

"If they're hurting you, I would be."

"You talked to Immie?"

His brows went up. "Don't change the subject. What's going on?"

"Nothing," she said on a sigh. "Someone asked me to do something."

"You don't want to do it?"

"I don't know."

"If you don't want to do it, don't do it," he said. "These things always start with one small step. You take that one step and another... Is this Steeple? Something he wants you to write about?"

Confirming that suspicion was better than telling the truth. "Sure," she said. "Steeple."

"You know how I felt about the Manzani thing," he said. "You're an incredible writer, but that won't mean anything if you're dead."

Something she'd considered in another circumstance. "You do difficult things. Dangerous things. All the time."

"I carry a badge and a gun," he said. "I can protect myself."

"And I'm just a feeble woman?"

He snickered. "Think I want my balls served to me on a plate? No, I don't think you're feeble. But I think guys like Vex know better than to take down a cop."

"I'm the sister of a cop," she said. "Did you tell Immie she was a feeble woman in need of protection?"

He laughed again. "See my previous answer. Immie's worse. She dives in headfirst. I want to think you're smarter than that."

"Because I learned so much from you?" she teased. "Maybe that's the problem. I want to do the right thing."

"So do it."

"You always told me that doing the right thing never starts with doing the wrong thing."

"And I was right."

"What if there's no other way out? Maybe the wrong thing is the only way."

"Don't buy it," he said.

"There are others involved."

"Whatever you want is right, Ser. And I know you, you don't want anyone to get hurt. If you want to do the right thing, you find a way to make it happen. No one can bully you. No one can make you do anything you don't want to do. If they try it, you come see me," he said, leaning back when the server brought their drinks.

"Thank you," she said when the woman left.

"For?"

"You're the only one who doesn't make me doubt myself."

Sometimes her mind was fried by the different people in her life demanding different things or giving opposing views. Lachlan didn't tell her what to think or what to do; he told her to trust herself.

"Don't need to," he said, picking up his glass. "I taught you well."

Yes, he had, and thank God for him.

TEN

ESCAPING IT WAS IMPOSSIBLE.

Maybe that was why she chose to wear her off-shoulder bandage dress in hot pink. She had to own her choice. Had to walk tall and stand proud... or he'd eat her alive.

Without even checking out her living room window, she went outside knowing the Bentley would be on the curb. Ire expected her to show up, mission complete.

She had a drink in the back of the car. Two... doubles...

Confidence. Certainty. She shouldn't doubt herself.

At the club, the car door opened, and she didn't wait for anyone's permission to go inside. Security moved out of her way at the door and at the stairs to allow her up.

People were beginning to expect her. Or the boss gave orders to let her in. Maybe some of his people were like her, dragooned and coerced against their will… or maybe not.

She went into the office, throwing the door back into the frame before anyone could follow her.

Ire and Niall stood on the rug, whiskey in the glasses they held. She marched on, opening her purse to retrieve the envelope.

She tossed it down on the desk. "I didn't do it."

Turning to face him, she expected a fight. He side-nodded at Niall, who put his glass down and departed. Seemed every time she walked in, he was sent out.

And they were alone again.

Their eyes met.

"Good," Ire said, sipping his drink.

"Good? Did you hear what I said?" she asked, putting her purse on the desk. "I didn't do it. There's your envelope, unopened. Babcock didn't get whatever you wanted me to deliver. How can you say that's good? You didn't want me to do it?"

After the emotional and mental turmoil of the day, she couldn't believe he'd be so glib.

"Means I won the bet with Niall."

Further taken aback, she retreated a step. "You didn't think I'd do it?"

Sinister glee narrowed his eyes. "Hoped you wouldn't."

Her blood cooled. "Why?"

"An alderman, the Police Superintendent, and one of the city's finest vice detectives," he said. "I get to take them out with the click of a button. It's a gift. Think how much easier my life gets when your family falls apart."

"You don't have to do it," she said, her heart pounding. Was she appealing to his sense of fairness? His decency? Neither had a hope with this guy, he wasn't capable. "You wanted to humiliate me? To make a point? Point made. I get it."

"No, but you will when the tape hits the wires."

He started to turn, but she grabbed his arm. "Please. There has to be another way."

He considered her. "You can't care that much. Why didn't you do it? Because you're stubborn? That was enough to sacrifice your family. Knew the night we met you had no loyalty. You didn't surprise me. I expect people to look out for themselves. Number one, that's what it's all about."

Mr. Know-It-All thought he was so smart. "Because it was illegal," she said, resenting the shit out of him. "I didn't do it because it was illegal."

"You didn't open it; how do you know?"

She didn't blink. "Am I wrong?"

And his lack of answer was answer enough. His body turned toward hers again. Her hand slid away as his rose to move a tendril of hair from her cheek.

"And if there was a legal option?"

A compromise? "I do something legal, and you give me the recording. Every copy. And don't hurt my family."

"You do something legal and I don't ruin your family."

"The recording?"

"Stays in my private collection until we reach the end of our agreement."

"Which will be when?"

"That depends."

"On?"

"When I'm finished with you."

"Me?" she asked and swallowed. "Just what is it you want?"

One corner of his mouth edged a fraction higher as his eyes darkened. "You." She swallowed again. "You give yourself to me. All of yourself. Every part of you and your life follows my rules."

"Sexually," she said, a frisson of excitement igniting though her better judgment screamed. "You want me to pander to your ego."

"You will do as you're told. When you're told. How you're told."

Unlikely. "It's sick. Forcing a woman to pleasure you. Do you really get off on that?"

His tongue pushed out his upper lip before sliding along it. "Do you need to watch our tape? This is your fantasy, baby."

A barb of resentful elation tumbled in her gut. How could he read her like her every defense was clear glass? Even the argument in her head seemed insincere. He did arouse her. Without a word, he'd turned her on and taken her to bed. No hitches, no objections. Even him shooting someone didn't put her off. What the hell was wrong with her?

She hadn't second-guessed herself. And, in truth, not one part of her regretted giving into him… until she saw the recording.

"Don't pretend you don't want it," he murmured, grazing her jaw with his fingertips. "You know you do. You feel it, in your pussy, right now. How much you want this… Want me. I'm giving you a gift, handing you a ticket to satisfy your deepest, darkest desires. We'll play and the only rule will be pleasure… Anything goes in this house, baby. You can have anything in my bed… anything." The tingle between her thighs pulsed, warming, waiting… eager. When she licked her lips, trying to get herself together, his touch floated across her pulse point to the swell of her breast. "I know you're wet for me, baby, ready for me to slide into your sweet, tight pussy… You want to be in my bed. This is what you want."

And damn, he was probably right. Blackmailing her was low, the lowest of the low, but her reaction to the notion of being in his bed didn't revolt her. It intrigued her.

"If I'm playing your girlfriend, doesn't that defeat the object?" she asked, trying to steady her voice. "I don't want the world to know—"

"My people wouldn't dare say a word about my personal life," he stated. "Any associate I see here keeps bigger secrets than who's in my bed. You came here every day for a month without worrying what the world would think. As far as the world is concerned, it's more of the same."

"You want me to come here every night?"

"Your concern should be that *I* come here every night." His lip almost rose, but it wasn't necessary. Satisfaction oozed from him. "If you don't please me, the deal will be off."

"I don't see how it can work."

He didn't share her uncertainty. "You'll follow orders, just like everyone else around here."

Every word out of his mouth was fact. No question. No doubt or indecision. Nothing but absolute confidence.

"Like an employee."

But with sex. Did she want him to win? To be manipulated with sex and debauchery? No. Not in theory. Strat said she wanted to be a part of the darkness. That it aroused her. And standing there, looking into the jade of his ominous eyes, she could forget all the negativity and feel the baser intoxication responsible for taking her to his bed in the first place.

More than that… she wanted to explore what he made her feel.

Professionally, it wouldn't hurt either. This McDade would make an interesting article. Steeple wanted more. Why not give it a shot? Yes, she'd investigate the mystery Strat gave her too, but the McDades were integral to that. Both stories complemented each other. It could work... even if the subject didn't know her objective.

"It's your choice," he said. "Consent or the video's released."

She hesitated for a beat, then took his glass. "Deal."

As she sipped the whiskey, he assessed her, moving a step closer. "Make me believe you, Sersha."

Though her heart was pounding, she took her time about putting down the drink. "If you want anyone to believe this..." She slipped her hands onto his shirt under his jacket, pressing just enough to appreciate the solid body beneath. "You have to let me be me." She got a little closer. "You might be in charge, but I'm no pushover."

He grabbed her hips to force her against his desk. "The real me doesn't take orders from a woman."

"Which may be why you have to blackmail them into sticking around."

As he'd done before, he tipped his head toward the door without unlocking their gazes. "Walk out," he said. "You're no one's prisoner."

"If I do that, everyone I care about loses everything."

"And that's a reason to sacrifice your freewill?" he asked, skimming his hands onto her waist, boosting her up to sit on his desk.

Her knees parted as he scooped her to the edge. Damn, how did they always end up...? Maybe her signals were the problem. She couldn't stop stroking him, her hands going higher and higher until they threatened to push his jacket off.

"You gave me no other choice."

"Is that what you need to believe?"

Maybe. Yes. That was exactly what she needed to believe, even as her fingers interlinked at the back of his neck to guide him closer.

"What is wrong with me?" she whispered, closing her eyes as the dizziness of endorphins loosened her muscles.

His breath stole hers, right there, his lips on the threshold of her mouth. "It tastes good."

Yes, it did, too good. "I'll never be able to trust you."

"I haven't lied to you yet."

Her eyes opened to meet his again. "You didn't tell me you were filming us having sex."

"That was an omission, not a lie." And for a man who ate immorality for breakfast, that was an important distinction. "Ask me a question and I will tell you the truth."

Fighting her primal urges wasn't easy; she'd never been so overcome. Still, certainty was important.

"Is that a promise?" she asked, still wary, and got a nod. "Are there any cameras or audio equipment recording here or upstairs right now?"

"No."

"Then how did you—"

"Upstairs are motion activated," he said. "No one's up there."

But if they went up, those cameras would turn on. "I won't have sex with you wherever there are cameras."

Why give him more evidence?

"I'll turn them off," he said, descending to almost meet her lips again. "If you ask nicely."

Nicely? She wanted to punch him in the eye.

Biting her tongue, she pushed him back, searching for sincerity. "I don't want to be filmed or recorded in any way. Can you promise that won't happen?"

"Not only can I promise it, but I can swear to obliterate any man who tries it." Tough talk. Shit, she stopped breathing when he leaned in. "McDades have power. We have reach. Being with me comes with benefits, Sersha." And he didn't mean in the bedroom. "Do your job right and I might let you take advantage of that. This is real. To anyone outside my circle, we're legit." Because he was using her to widen his net of legitimate contacts, she was no fool. "Understand?"

Was that a threat? What did being with a man like him mean? Smiling at him in front of others? Laughing at his jokes… if he made jokes.

"No advantage will save me from your bed, will it?" she asked. "You'll still expect me to lie on my back for you."

"I expect a helluva lot more than that."

"And I'm just supposed to accept your word? How can I accept your word you're not filming every second we spend together?"

"I've got you on the hook. Squirm, baby, makes no difference. I have no reason to lie. The cameras are off 'cause that's what I want. If I wanted them on, they'd be on. Ask and I'll tell you the truth. But I have all the footage I need to tighten your chain."

"And if you decide you want to record us again?"

"Then I will."

"And what?"

"When we're done, you walk away with anything intimate or incriminating."

"I can't trust you."

"Okay," he said, pulling her arms away to step back. "Daly will take you home."

Which meant her family's pain. Plenty of journalists went deep for the right story. Was the risk worth it? As he said, he already had enough to pull the trigger. Even if he recorded every other encounter, all it would mean was more embarrassment for her. The damage would be the same. Her words, she'd be careful with those, but the physical? The horse had already bolted on that score.

"No," she said, sliding off the desk. "What do I have to lose? You already have all the power."

Though he grew more discerning, his exhale was gruff enough to be amusement. "Flattery?"

"Girl's got to get through the day," she said, stroking down his arm to guide it around her as she stepped in against him. "Last time we got close down here, someone got shot."

"He survived."

"So you want to take another shot?" she asked, tucking a hand under his jacket again. "Or take this somewhere else?"

"I have a meeting."

"And I heard you were one for breaking rules…"

As he dipped lower, he squeezed her ass and tipped her chin to join their mouths. Whoever she was trying to convince, there was no lie in her natural response to those lips massaging hers. Maybe it was his force, the unapologetic demand of his tongue conquering her mouth. Within seconds, she was clinging to the fabric on his body, pressing her own against him.

She didn't hear the door opening, but he must've because he broke the kiss to turn. There was Babcock on the threshold, Niall just behind him, and someone beyond.

"Any weapons around?" Niall asked, obviously thinking of what happened last time.

"Mr. McDade," Babcock said, his eyes widening. "I didn't mean—we think—"

"It's okay," she said, avoiding Ire's eyes when they came around to hers.

"Upstairs to bed," he growled down at her, squeezing her ass. She just nodded and wiped the smudge of her lip gloss from his mouth. His arm loosened to let her go. As she turned, she paused to tip the whiskey from one glass to the other, taking it and her purse with her. Something had to keep her company as she came to terms with the change. She reached for the curtain. "Ser…" Pausing, she peeked over her shoulder. "You like anything you're wearing, lose it before I get up there."

The curve of her lips was honest. How could she not be flattered by that implication? Disappearing around the curtain, she ascended the stairs into Ire's private space.

It was unlikely he meant the tease. Babcock was there, they had an audience. Oh, God, what had she gotten herself into? McDade was in charge and, until he said otherwise, she was his plaything.

As far as the McDade world was concerned, their relationship was mutual. She could play to that. It was a game. Nothing between them was real… was it?

TO BE CONTINUED...

READ ON FOR A SNEAK PEEK FROM THE NEXT BOOK…

ONE

POUNCING ONTO HER elbows, Sersha awoke suddenly.

Bed low to the floor, black satin sheets, stag heads embroidered in the corner of the pillowcases. Stag. Ire McDade's nightclub. His private bedroom. Their deal. Sex for silence.

Except she was alone.

"McDade," she whispered, touching her lips.

What happened? She'd done as told, stripped off and slipped into his bed, then waited and waited… Apparently, he'd never arrived.

Casting the sheet aside, she got up to check the

closet. No one. Her hand brushed along the hanging clothes until she snagged a shirt to button it over her bare body.

In the bathroom… Still no one. And no steam or water droplets to suggest recent use.

Leaving by the second door, she rounded into the long living space. A large segmented semi-circular window at the other end let in daylight.

Passing between the seating area and stocked bar, she skirted the dining table to peek outside. No one was out there either. The kitchen by the window tempted her closer. Drinks in the fridge, coffee, nothing to eat. Padded stools, better suited for a bar than a kitchen island, suggested they used the space for entertaining rather than as a full-time residence.

What kind of home would a man like Ire McDade live in?

And where had he gone? Last night she'd assumed he would come to her in bed and hadn't asked for further instructions. Whatever he expected, he hadn't been explicit, and there was no way she'd hang around all day waiting and wondering.

Real or not, she took a shower and put her dress back on, pairing it with one of Ire's suit jackets. For warmth. And to hide the morning-after shame. Not that there had been a night-before. Wasn't sex what he wanted? Why demand complete sexual submission only to pass up the chance to exploit it?

He didn't seem like the type to flake on someone. Or the type to sleep next to a sexually accessible woman and keep his hands off. Unless he'd changed his mind about their deal. Shit. What would that mean for their sex tape? Could it already be out there?

Dread became more real in the vacant office. From the internal windows there, she checked out the club below. Empty too.

Being alone was eerie. Everything looked different bathed in the sun streaming through the glazed roof panels. She hadn't even known they existed. With the club lights and the night always above, she'd never given the ceiling much thought.

The office wasn't locked. Good. At least she wasn't a prisoner. No one stood on the stairs, or even at the bottom of them. Where was security? Off-duty? Had she slept through the apocalypse?

The club entrance was closed. No big deal, except how did she open such massive doors? They folded back, maybe, hinges in the middle—a smaller section opened in from the outside before she got that far. What the hell? Another thing she'd never noticed. A door within a door.

Stepping outside, past the guy who'd opened the door, her focus stuck on her McDade protector, Daly, waiting by the Bentley at the curb.

"Going to work?" he asked, opening the back door.

"Home first," she said, frowning when he held the takeout coffee cup toward her. "What is that?"

"Venti hazelnut latte, skinny, extra shot."

She laughed, taking the cup from him to sniff the steam. "How do you know my coffee?"

"Normal day is breaking kneecaps and noses collecting cash," he said. "Getting a guy to spill on your coffee order is cake."

Uh… "Okay."

Ducking into the car, the door closed behind her, and she sipped the coffee. Nothing was as she expected. No sex but protection, a driver, and the perfect coffee. What game was McDade playing?

***

WORK HAD A WAY of focusing her. After too many hours in The Chronicler basement archives, she needed to get out of the building. If she didn't breathe fresh air at regular intervals, she got pretty myopic.

Outside, the Bentley was waiting. Just… waiting. Daly got out as she approached.

"I don't need the car. I'm going to a deli down the block," she said, looking up and down the street. "Are you allowed to park there all day?"

"Think some beat cop's gonna challenge us?" Maybe. Maybe not. "Need me to come with you?"

"No," she said, smiling as she retreated. "You want anything?"

He shook his head, so she turned to lose herself in the bustle of people. They didn't matter. She was too in her own head. Facts and possibilities whizzed around in her mind.

McDade and Manzani. Maybe it wasn't wise to squeeze herself in between two families like theirs.

Her boss, Steeple, wanted her to build on the exposé piece she'd written about the Manzani family. Then her friend and source, Strat, tantalized her with a decades old McDade mystery. As an investigative reporter, she couldn't ignore the intrigue.

A McDade was missing. A McDade woman… and they were rare.

Connel's cousin. Did he know her? Remember her? She'd been gone a long time. Maybe they'd never met. Maybe she was long dead. And that was the mystery. What happened to Dorsey McDade?

In the deli, she ordered and sat at a table, all the while texting. Her brother. Strat. Steeple.

"Which one is it?"

The male voice drew her attention up, but the speaker was already sinking into the perpendicular chair.

"Evander," she said, every muscle tensing.

Evander "Vex" Manzani. Her not-so-secret admirer. Son of Don Silvio Manzani who ran most any part of the city Ire didn't.

"You get my flowers?" he asked, sliding a hand over hers. "You and your games, baby."

Why was he smiling?

Shit, that never led to anything good. "I'm not playing games." She withdrew from his touch. "How many times do I have to say it, Evander?"

"I love this play," he said, picking up her hand. "Shit, you love stirring it up. Staying all night at McDade's club...? Fuck, I thought you'd lost your mind, screwing that bastard. I'd fight that war for my princess, but talk about going nuclear."

"I'm not your princess," she said, dragging her hand from his again. "We've talked about this. This is not a game."

"That Irish scum..." he said like she hadn't spoken at all. "It's gotta be one of his guys... You want me to take them out one by one 'til I hit the one you fucked last night? I'll spill their blood for you. I'll play this out, right to the end."

His palm skimmed her arm; disgust prickled beneath it.

"Evander," she said, pacing a slow breath. "I don't want any blood spilled. What I was doing last night is none of your business. Are your people still following me?"

There was no other way he could know she'd spent the night at Stag.

"They expected you to come out. Every night you do... until last night. That fuck McDade is beneath you, beneath us, but his people... why the fuck...? Why degrade yourself? Is it blackmail? Have they got something on you? Why fuck with his guys?"

"I'm not. I wouldn't."

"McDade left with a blonde and a redhead after two," he said. Lucky women. "He know you were in his place fucking his guys?"

Keeping her face still, an odd curl of jealousy grew barbs in her belly. "Stop this. It isn't healthy for either of us."

"It's our curse," he said, his hand reaching the side of her neck. "Wanting each other."

"You can't keep doing this," she said. "Showing up like this. Someone will get hurt." Thank God Daly hadn't joined her or there would've been carnage. The deli people didn't deserve that. No one did. "Did you come in the front?"

If Daly saw…

"I know what you want," he said, dragging his chair closer, prompting her to look away. Why did he have to get so close? Sickness churned in her gut. When his lips touched her shoulder, she recoiled and whipped around, ready to lash out. But she couldn't. With a guy like Evander, there was a careful line to tread. "You want to keep it secret? Fuck with him behind his back?"

No, she really didn't, but this guy never heard her. "Evander—"

"This weekend, it's time to do this," he said. "Tomorrow night, Platinum Suite."

"What?"

He stood and bent over to kiss her hair. "Midnight."

Fading toward the back of the deli, he disappeared through an employee door.

Midnight. Friday. He wasn't suggesting… Except there, on the table by her coffee, was a key card bearing the Grand Hotel's logo.

Shit.

TWO

BACK IN THE archives that afternoon, putting together the McDade family tree complicated her attempts to rid Ire from her mind. Tough not to think about the guy when reading his name every twenty seconds.

Should she tell him about her conversation with Evander in the deli? Should she not? Ire assumed she'd chosen Stag for protection. Yes, fine, true. That didn't mean she'd ever intended for their paths to cross. Yet, somehow, not only had she got the McDades involved in her mess, but she'd ended up holding the detonator between the two factions.

Okay, so the families wouldn't be breaking bread anytime soon; that wasn't on her. But there was a tentative peace between the McDades and the Manzanis. Each had their own territories, their own strengths. They stayed away from each other's business as much as possible. By all outward appearances anyway.

How many news reports had she read that day? Hundreds? Thousands? However many it was, by the time she left The Chronicler building, it was dark out, and she didn't feel any wiser.

"Thought you'd ditched us again," Daly said, opening her car door. "Stag?"

"Home."

Before she could get in, he pushed the door to block her way. "Boss is expecting you."

And that was part of the deal.

"I'm hungry," she said. "And I'd bet he doesn't want me showing up without taking a shower and changing my clothes."

"An hour, max.," he said, determined, widening the ingress again.

"Did he say something?" she asked. "If he's giving you shit, just tell him the truth. I'm working. I have to do my job."

"This started as watching Manzani's mark."

One related to the other, how? "I don't—"

"Watching the boss's woman is a different gig. A whole different ballgame."

She smiled, ready to dismiss his concern. "Yeah, but it's not—"

Wait. Did Daly know about the deal? He had to know the relationship wasn't real. Didn't he? Hmm, best ask Connel and get some clarity on who knew what.

Daly stayed serious. "I have a job to do too."

Even if Daly was aware the relationship was a sham, others weren't. Did being Ire McDade's woman put her in a different kind of jeopardy? Avoiding Evander was one thing. Being queen in the hornet's nest was a new angle that could lead to worse trouble.

No one else should take heat for her choices. "I'll talk to him."

"You don't want to do that," he said.

"I don't?"

He shook his head and gestured inside. "Fifty-nine minutes."

Okay, right, he wanted to get moving. Now she did too. She and Ire needed to have a conversation.

***

THE EMBROIDERED NARROW straps of her red dress descended into a plunge that revealed her cleavage. It was just lucky she had a thing for buying dresses. Both her work and family lives required her to attend a bunch of functions, giving her plenty of excuses to splurge.

Haste. Yes, Daly wanted her to be quick. Still, things took as long as they took. More than an hour passed while she cooked, showered, and prettied herself for Stag. Her routine was the same as always… wasn't it? Okay, so she lingered over hair and makeup, and even did her nails. Either she cared about impressing Ire or was delaying the inevitable.

Both were probably true.

By the time the car pulled up to Stag, necessity drove her on. She got out with purpose in her step. How often was that purpose played through to the end? Never. Each time, Ire pulled the rug out from under her, and she ended up flat on her back. Literally. Being around him got her dizzy. Getting close… too close…

It wouldn't happen again. She'd have a drink, screw her head on straight, and complete her objective.

Guards at the foot of the stairs to the office moved aside, but her trajectory remained the same. Going straight past them, she strode on into the club. Something about the music grounded her. As always, the club delivered. Oblivion. Anonymity. Safe harbor.

Everyone needed to forget their lives sometimes. Forget who they were and everything going on around them. How could her life have become such a hot mess?

She ordered a drink and sat at the bar, pretending

nothing was different. Like she could just sit there, protected by the surrounding shell, the illusion of safety.

"Let me get that for you."

Fuck. A guy. A random guy. It never failed.

Her shoulders dropped as she exhaled. "No, thank you."

The guy, whoever he was, it didn't matter, sidled up close. Too close for a woman who wanted to be alone.

"Back up there, buddy."

Daly. He must've followed her because there he was, right behind her.

"Just talking to the lady."

"Yeah, you don't want to do that." Daly's arm came down on the bar between her and the guy she hadn't even looked at. "Back up."

"Who are you?" the guy asked. "She your girlfriend?"

Daly's head turned her way to murmur. "You don't want to do this, Sersha." The warning came in his words and his serious gaze. "They call him Ire for a reason."

"Hey, dude…" the guy said.

The bartender came over with her drink. "Daly, there a problem?"

Daly's eyes stayed on hers. "No problem, Biggs. Right, Sersha? Tell Biggs there's no problem."

Drawing in a breath, she picked up her drink. "No. No problem."

Her leash was short.

As she slipped off the stool, Daly's protective arm closed around her waist, guiding her through the tables, toward the exit again. But there was no reprieve. The security guys stepped out of the way to let them ascend the stairs toward the office.

"Playing with him isn't like playing with other guys," Daly hissed.

"I wasn't playing with anyone," she said. "Can't a girl just want a drink?"

"There's a fully stocked bar upstairs," he said, stopping at the top, holding the door handle. "You want a bartender up there? Just say the word." Their eyes met again. "But you cannot be around other guys like that. Women don't leave McDades. And you sure don't screw around on Ire McDade."

"Because Ire has a rep to protect?"

"Not for his sake."

"Mine?"

"Theirs," he said and edged in closer. "Shit, Sersha, you understand what he's capable of, right? He shot Dingo for walking in on you two together. What do you think a guy they call 'Ire' will do to any man who touches you? Who flirts with you? Who buys you a drink?"

Concern brought her brows closer. "Are you telling me to be afraid of him?"

"I'm telling you to be afraid *for* them. You want to fuck around with other guys? Their injuries, their deaths, will be on you."

She blinked in surprise. "Their deaths? You're exaggerating… aren't you?"

He snickered in contradiction. Someone pulled the door from his hand, opening it from the other side.

Niall stood there before them. "Just her. We're going out," he said to Daly, who turned to descend again. "Miss McLeod."

The acknowledgement came with Niall putting a hand on her lower back to push her inside. He closed the door behind her.

Ire was at the desk, on the phone, fixated on something in the corner. As she went a few steps, the long nook opposite his position opened up. The two blondes were on the chesterfield again. Sans clothes.

"Bring her…" Ire said into the phone, beckoning her with two straight fingers and pointing at the chair at the end of his desk. He smiled as his attention drifted, but it wasn't for her. "Make you no promises… I've heard…" She went to sit, putting the glass and her purse on the desk. "Not sure I do. Your Doherty puts on a show…" His light tone wasn't typical. Was it the blondes? Them enjoying each other seemed to be his focus. "I was there that night… Think every guy did…"

The blondes were beautiful, no denying it. Long silky hair. Perfect skin. What was it men enjoyed about women enjoying each other? Not that she judged them. Having never been with a woman, she couldn't say whether it would be satisfying to touch one like the pair on the couch touched each other.

Over the years, more than a dozen men had groped her. They'd used their hands and fingers to please her. She was used to men's bodies. The hard angles. The ridge of their arousal. How it felt to be filled by them.

The touch of his lips on her shoulder startled her. Was he finished on the phone? She tried to turn on a smile. With the women present, they couldn't talk about their situation, their deal, or about Evander.

Ire's narrow eyes stayed close, his lips a breath from her shoulder. What was it with men kissing her there?

Looking into him, a weight of need settled over her. Tired suddenly, but not in need of sleep, she licked her lips, aching to feel his against her again.

"Did I interrupt?" she asked, reaching for some semblance of sanity.

"My cousin."

That was a shock. The blondes, over there…

"They're your cousins?"

"On the phone," he said, sweeping her hair from her shoulder as he stood up.

Good, because that would be weird. Creepy… Perverted. They didn't look Irish either. Scandinavian? Russian? What did she know? Ire's father had dark hair. He looked just like him; she'd been looking at pictures of McDades all day. The women over there, kissing, touching, they didn't have the family's authority. Even in 2D, the McDades presented formidable figures.

Yet, something about the women entranced her. She couldn't tear her eyes away. Did they enjoy being on show? A hand on a breast slid lower. Sensing it, the second woman parted her thighs, moving into the caress.

"Want to join them?"

She jumped. How could she be unaware of him when he was her reason for being there?

His question filtered in and she breathed out an awkward laugh. "No. God, no."

"You're used to living with rules," he said, rounding the desk, whiskey in hand, to prop himself on the corner, observing the women too. "Those rules don't exist here, Sersha. Learn to be a bad girl. Satisfy your curiosity."

That lilt, the way he said her name, even that didn't quite land right. Mesmerized by the delicate fingers sliding through soft hair, the allure tempted her.

"I wouldn't—I mean I've never…" Her mouth dried. His glass landed on the desk, then his open hand was in front of her. "What?"

She slipped her hand into his and with one tug, he pulled her to her feet. His other hand drifted up her arm, along her clavicle to her throat.

"We don't need a reason to do something in this house," he said. The back of his finger ascended the front of her neck to ease her chin higher. He ducked to kiss her slow. No tongue, just a long, gentle press of his lips to hers. Her eyes stayed closed when his mouth ebbed. "We need a reason not to do it… No one expects you to be a good girl here. You don't need to behave. What reason is there to resist what feels good?"

TO BE CONTINUED...

Thank you for reading this tale!
If you can, please take the time to review.

~

Ask your local library for more Scarlett Finn novels!

~

For all things Scarlett Finn check out:

www.scarlettfinn.com

BOOK TWO

SCARLETT FINN

OUT NOW!

www.ingramcontent.com/pod-product-compliance
Lightning Source LLC
Chambersburg PA
CBHW030809190726
48285CB00003B/1087